Written By

# Don't be scared
# of who you are!

Illustrations
Zoe Pennent

About the author:

I'm Sulayma Nourdeen and I am a 12 year old girl. From the time I was a little girl I've always had books and I would read them all the time; I think I was naturally a bookworm. I love reading and story writing; that is what makes me happy.

My inspiration for writing this book was my stepmum Zoe. When I read her book "11 Pathways to Healing Myself", I thought to myself that if she can write her own books and publish it, then so could I.

Another thing that really inspired me to write this book was Emily the main character, throughout writing the book I could visualise everything, and it made me feel like I was really there with her.

Thanks

I would like to thank my stepmum
Zoe for doing all my illustrations
for my book and helping me
develop and create the book, also
for believing in me to finish it.

I would also like to thank my mum
and family for encouraging me to
do the book and finish it and for
also having faith in me.

Don't Be Scared Of Who You Are

Introduction

This book "Don't Be Scared Of Who You Are" is about a 12 year old girl called Emily Smith.

Emily Smith had a hard time growing up as a child and making friends was not any easier. Emily hopes now that she has got a new family and lives in a new house and area things will be different and people will like her for the way she is.

Are you ready to read on about Emily's difficult life of making friends and all sorts? If so, you'd better continue reading to see what happens!

A Hard Time Growing Up

September 26th 2019

Hello, I'm Emily Smith and this is my life. Growing up has not been fun including the start of my life but do not worry; you won't miss out on anything because I am here to take you through it step by step.

I was born on April the 17th 2008 in Mayday Hospital at approximately 2:56 in the morning. Some people say I am bad luck due to my mum passing away 4 days after giving birth to me.

I am not sure why my mum passed away; was I that ugly that people were making me out to be so? Did she not like me, or did she not want me? My dad tells me all the time that it is not my fault that my mum passed away and that she had difficulties giving birth to me, but dad can't stop me from wondering like any other kid would.

When my mum died my dad got really depressed and started

going out late by himself, leaving me alone in the house with nothing to do. Me and my dad did not have a strong relationship and we never really talked; I thought that is how it was meant to be with parents.

My dad got worse and I mean really bad that he started coming home walking all funny, talking all funny and believe it or not, acting all funny. I had never seen my dad like this before and so it really scared me, and I had no clue what to do.

I go to sleep at night wondering what it would be like if mum was here. Would my dad ever go back to normal? Would he ever be the same again? And would I ever have a true family that cares and loves me and doesn't treat me how my dad does.

School, School ,School

September 28th 2019

School is so difficult with all this English, Maths and Science. Do we really need to know all of that at our young ages? Also, it's not just that some of the teachers are annoying, and I mean really annoying to the point where I can't handle them no more!

Well, I have to be honest it's not just that...I have no friends and you are most likely thinking you must at least have one friend! But no, not a single soul! I never knew why I had no friends; was I really that hard to like? That's probably why me and my dad don't have a relationship right?

People don't like me, and I don't know why. Is it the way I look or the way I dress? I'm not sure; they never told me. It is bad enough me having to go to a school where I don't belong or fit in, but there are these really mean people that bully me everyday.

The people that bullied me are really horrible and their names are Rubi, Tiana and Rose. They treat me badly because everyday when I come into my lessons, all of them trip me up purposely and just laugh at me as I struggle. Like they have nothing better to do!

No matter how many times I tell my teachers about it they never do anything and that really upsets me because I don't think anyone should be treated like that as a matter of fact. I am starting to think that my school does not care that I am getting bullied because they would have done something about it and they have not.

It was nearly the end of my English lesson and I was packing up all my stationery and books, when my English teacher told me to sit back down and wait until everyone else left the classroom. To no surprise, the mean girls started laughing at me but once again Ms just told me to ignore them.

Ms Lovely slowly made her way over to my table and calmly sat down on the chair next to mine; Ms Lovely is the only one that has been nice and caring towards me since I started this school and I know I said I don't have any friends, but I think I might have one. This is how our conversation went:

"Emily what's wrong, you did not seem yourself today at all?"

"It's just that these girls are always mean to me and they never get into trouble!"

"I know they don't get into trouble and it's not right that they don't but you see I don't have much power in this school, but like I always say to you, don't let the haters get you down because that's what they want!"

"Thanks Ms Lovely you are so kind and caring, thank you for everything you have done for me; I am really grateful."

"You are so welcome Emily, and you know where I am if you need to talk anytime ok."

Yes Ms Lovely, I know; thank you!"

My English teacher slowly rose from her chair and walked away turning her head to me for one more glance at me with a thumbs up.

I gathered up the rest of my belongings whilst thinking about everything Ms lovely had said to me; it just went round and round in my head like it could not find a way out.

Carefully, I pick up my school bag and put it on my back and walk out of the room slowly with my head bowed to the floor like I had just got into trouble or ashamed of something. Making my way out of school is the best feeling in the world as I don't have to deal with the three musketeers anymore. I make my way home singing songs on the pavement kicking stones as I go along, like I am happy to be going home and that other kids would accept me, because I don't have a loving caring family like others do.

# Trouble

## September 29th 2019

I am in trouble; I am panicking. I got home from school yesterday and my dad was not home; I waited and waited outside the house but he did not come home. Suddenly, I realised that my dad always kept a spare key under the mat. Making my way into the house shivering like crazy I was so scared because the house was empty. No one was there and that is what scared me the most! I just could not do it, I just couldn't so I ran to my room in a flash and slammed the door behind me.

I ran to my bed, stuck my head under the pillow and cried as loud as I could; I was petrified that I had no plan. I had nothing to do or say until I heard some loud banging on the front door. I did not dare open it as I am not allowed to, but what could I do? Who was at the door? Was it my dad?

Shortly afterwards, the banging faded but was I safe? How would I know for sure they would not come back for more to try and scare me? It soon became 6:00pm and this is the time I normally eat my dinner but I assume there is none, as my dad is not here. I begin to look and scurry around my room for any food that I could eat that could be my dinner just for today (hopefully).

I found a Twix in my drawer that looked perfectly healthy to eat; I unwrapped the chocolate and shoved it down my throat like I had not eaten in a week. I was craving for more food as I was starving. I was thirsty...I was all of those things! Times like this I wish my dad was here even for just a minute.

Laying in my bed wide awake all night I hoped that I would hear my dad come through the door coming to comfort me, apologising for what happened. That was just a figment of my imagination. I know deep down he would never do that for me.

I know my dad was upset from my mum's death but I did not think he would ever get this bad and leave me alone in the house where I could be in massive danger with no adult around, especially at night!

My dad had never done this to me before and I was starting to get worried. Was my dad even ok? Did he choose not to come home to his daughter tonight or did someone take him? I'm going crazy right now! That could never happen to my dad; he is too strong!

My imagination is going crazy right now. I am thinking about positives and negatives that might have happened, but mostly negatives. All I can say right now is I have had enough. My dad has treated me badly since the day he started going out late. I am not going to have it anymore and am going to tell a teacher at school on Monday and that's that!

## Pain but Relief

### October 1st 2019

I am scared out of my bones about how I am going to be able to tell Ms Lovely about my dad? What if she cant help me? What if no one could help me? What would I do then?

Walking into school was embarrassing due to me shaking so much that people were staring and laughing at me. I did not dare look up as I knew I would start crying, So I just kept my head low. To my surprise Ms Lovely saved me by bumping into me and I had no choice but to look up. As soon as she witnessed the tears in my eyes, she took me to her office immediately to sit and chat.

When we reached her office, I thought to myself that this is the perfect opportunity to tell Ms Lovely what had been going on in my life as we were in her office and the door was shut, and no one was around to hear my shameful life.

Ms lovely smiled at me trying to comfort me, I guess to make me feel better and it was totally working, so I started to open up to her. This is how it went:

"Ms lovely if I tell you this, can you promise to help me?"

"Yes, I will Emily. I promise to help you in every way I can. So, what is the matter?"

"When I was born my mum passed away 4 days later. My dad got really depressed and started going out late and coming back all drunk and it really scared me."

"Oh my days Emily, how long has this been going on for?"

"A very long time....".

"This is not a safe environment for you to stay in. Is that all that happened?"

"No Ms, when I went home on Friday my dad was not there and I waited outside for a really long time and he did not come, and then I realised he kept a spare key under the mat so I went inside. Soon after, loud banging came on my front door but I did not dare to open it. All I have eaten over the weekend is a Twix bar and he is still not back."

"I am so sorry that all of this has happened to you. That is not right at all and I can help you. I can also call up some people too."

"Thank you so much Ms, all I want is a proper family that loves and cares for me."

"I know Emily, this is what every child wants and deserves. But for now I am going to have to speak to the headteacher because you cannot go back to that home."

"Thank you! But then where am I supposed to go after school?"

"You are going to have to stay with us a little bit longer than usual, and then someone nice and caring will come and get you and explain everything that is going to take place in proper detail. Is that ok?"

"Yes that is fantastic, but is it going to be scary?"

"It might be at first because you don't know the people, but you will adjust to love them as much as they love you."

"Thank you Ms for all your help and reassurance. I am truly grateful!"

"You are so welcome but you best start making your way to your lesson as you don't want to be late and I will go and speak with the headteacher."

"Thank you Ms."

As we wrap up our conversation I realise that telling Ms everything that has happened was a good thing because now I can get all the love and support I need, and most importantly a loving and caring family.

I made my way to my lesson with a smile on my face and with my head held up high with happiness. I haven't felt this way in a long time and I was happy that it was back. The reason why I am so happy is because I know I would never feel unwanted or uncared about again, because I was moving on with a new chapter in my life.

As I walk into my class, my teacher looks shocked to see me

smiling but I don't blame her because I have not smiled in school in a long time. Ms Abrams tells me to take my seat and I joyfully walk over to my chair and get all my supplies out for this lesson.

My main thought throughout the whole day was who was my new family, what they are like, if they would they like me, if they would accept me for who I am, and whether it is a couple and last but not least, if they have kids.

I had so many questions and was kind of annoyed by the fact that

I had to wait till the end of the day till I met this lady to see and know the answers, which irritated me.

In the middle of my last lesson of the day, Ms lovely came to the classroom to collect me to take me to the head teachers office. In my head I thought this was it and I could finally have a brand new loving caring family.

Me and Ms Lovely walked down the school corridor in complete silence like I had just got into trouble (which I had not). After a short walk we reached Ms Gabil's office; Ms looked down at me with a smile and I shot one right back at her.

Entering Ms Gabil's office and seeing a young lady sitting at her desk was my idea of fun and exciting news just for me. The lady turned around as she heard the door open and gave me a nice big smile!

Ms Gabils told me to take a seat and that the young lady was going to ask me some questions and explain to me what was going to happen. I was ready as I sat down as fast as I could and said in my head, "Here goes nothing."  But this is what was said:

"Hello Emily, I am Emma and I am here to ask you some questions and just explain to you what is going to happen from here on, is that ok?"

"Yes it is".

"So first of all how do you feel about going to live with a new family, and do you and your dad have a strong relationship?"

"No, me and my dad do not have a strong relationship and we never talk. I am really excited to move and live with a new family though."

"Why did you not tell anyone what was going on at home with your dad?"

"Because I was scared that they would judge me."

"I am sorry about that Emily".

"It's ok you don't need to be sorry."

"So, are you aware about what is going to happen?"

"No, so can you please explain?"

"Yes I can. So what is going to happen today is that you are going to go and stay with some people until your new family is ready for you, and then you will move to live with them. You will also have a Social Worker that will come and visit you and take you out to places and make sure everything is good with your new family and home."

"Yay I am really excited! Do you know the names of the people I am going to be staying with today?"

"Yes, their names are Jamie and Stacy".

"Will I still go to this school?"

"No, sadly because your new family doesn't live round here, sorry."

"It's ok, I don't mind; that's what I wanted anyway."

"One more thing, do you have any belongings like clothes or toys you would like to bring with you?"

"No, I don't have any clothes except for my uniform and I have never had toys".

"Ok that's fine, your new family can get you all of that. Would you like to get all your stuff and come with me?"

"Yes I would".

"I am feeling overjoyed from now knowing all this new information and I am extremely excited to meet my new family soon

Jamie and Stacy

October 2nd 2019

As you know Jamie and Stacy are not my real new family but they are really nice people and I must say their food is delicious.

Jamie and Stacy make me feel welcome and loved. They even tuck me in at night and give me a hug which has never happened to me before, and that really made me feel welcome. They also accepted me into their home even if it was not for long.

At the weekend when Jamie went to work, Stacy made these amazing pancakes with chocolate and blueberries. Stacy even took me shopping that day to get me new clothes and pyjamas and you can't forget my slippers which were so cosey as well!

Being here has made me realise how much of my childhood I have missed out on and I felt awful that I did not tell someone sooner.

On a wonderful evening when I was playing with my toys in my room, Stacy and Jamie both called me down into the living room to talk; I was kind of confused as I had not done anything wrong. When I reached the living room, I sat on the floor and they said to me they had great news. As soon as I heard that, a massive smile came upon my face as I knew I was not in trouble. This was the good news and how it went:

"Emily, your new family is ready for you and your Social Worker is going to come and pick you up tomorrow and take you there. Are you excited?"

"Yes I am. I am very excited! Thank you Jamie and Stacy for everything you guys have done for me."

"You are so welcome Emily. We know you will go on to have a bright future."

"I saw tears in their eyes so I went and gave them another big hug and thanked them again. We then we went to pack all of my stuff up in my room whilst having the time of our lives as it was my last night with them."

The Thompson Family

October 10th 2019

It has been a long time since I wrote in this diary! But that is because I have finally got my new family and we are called the Thompson family, and I must say they are all nice and caring towards me.

The Thompson Family honestly love me as they spoil me sometimes. The people in this family are:

Maddie - Mum

Tom - Dad

Alice - Sister

Thomas - Brother

Poppy - Dog

I love this family so much because
they are funny, kind and caring;
all that I had wished for. I go to
a new school now called St Mark's
school. I actually have so many
friends and they are all so nice to
me, and I am now a school
counsellor and that is fantastic if
I do say so myself!

The start of my life was not good
at all and I was having a really bad

and hard times, but everyone deserves a happy ending and that is exactly what I got!  With my new family and friends my life is practically amazing right now and it will stay like that, because I know that I have got the power and the strength to fight for my rights and a happy life.

Me signing off

Emily Thompson

Printed in Great Britain
by Amazon